THE
BET

RENICA REGO

notionpress.com

INDIA · SINGAPORE · MALAYSIA

Notion Press

No.8, 3rd Cross Street,
CIT Colony, Mylapore,
Chennai, Tamil Nadu – 600004

First Published by Notion Press 2021
Copyright © Renica Rego 2021
All Rights Reserved.

ISBN 978-1-63669-660-7

This book has been published with all efforts taken to make the material error-free after the consent of the author. However, the author and the publisher do not assume and hereby disclaim any liability to any party for any loss, damage, or disruption caused by errors or omissions, whether such errors or omissions result from negligence, accident, or any other cause.

While every effort has been made to avoid any mistake or omission, this publication is being sold on the condition and understanding that neither the author nor the publishers or printers would be liable in any manner to any person by reason of any mistake or omission in this publication or for any action taken or omitted to be taken or advice rendered or accepted on the basis of this work. For any defect in printing or binding the publishers will be liable only to replace the defective copy by another copy of this work then available.

For the one who deciphers my silence.

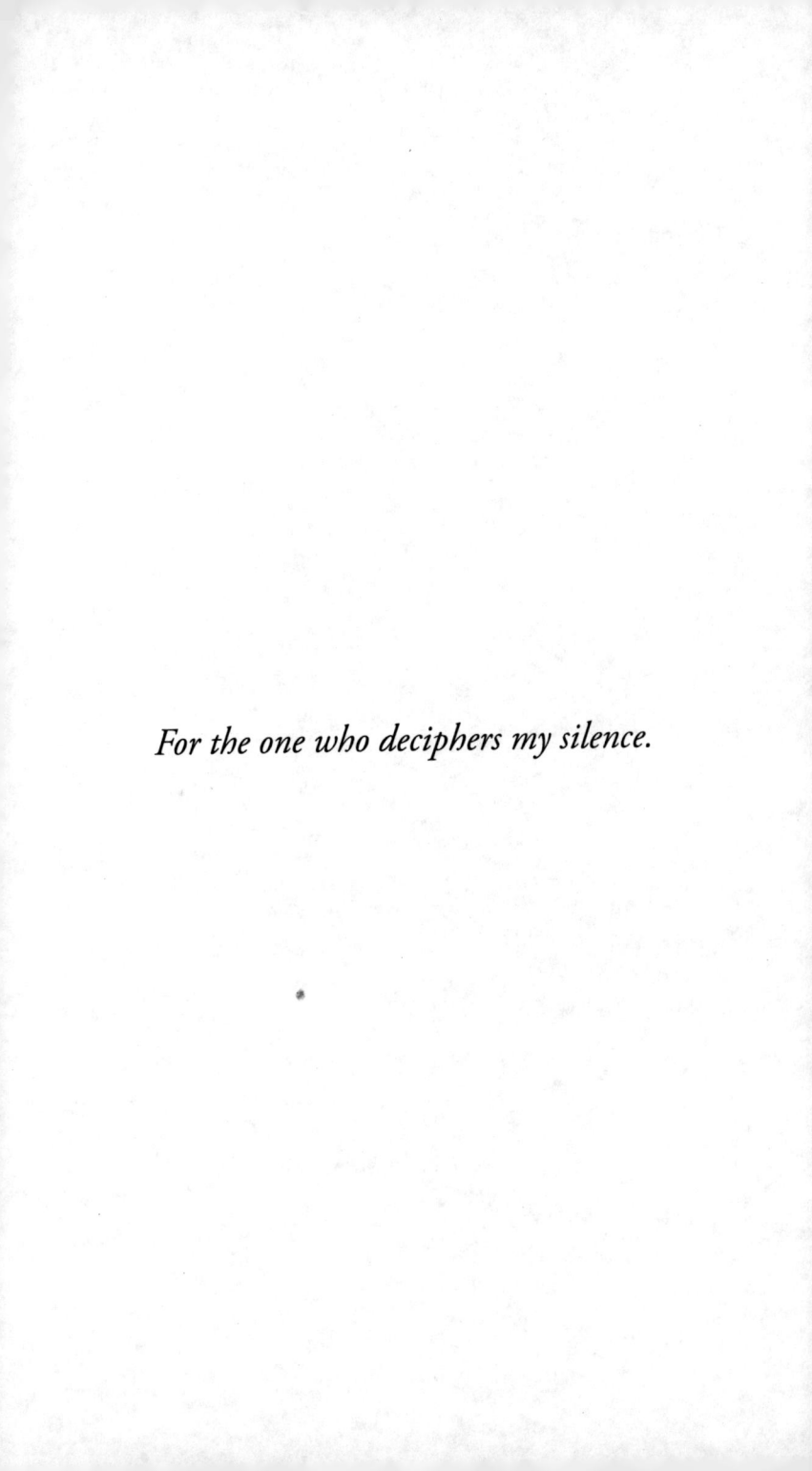

CONTENTS

Prologue   7

1. Misty Meadows   9
2. Losing Fingerprints   12
3. A Deliberate Life   15
4. The Importance of Being Beautiful   18
5. Wander More Often   21
6. The Lighthouse   25
7. Saved by a Song   29
8. Like a Lotus Leaf   32
9. The Silence between   35
10. Table for One   39
11. Into the Forest   42
12. The Silver Oak   45
13. A Case for Love   50
14. Yugen   53
15. Wabi Sabi Life   56
16. The Silent String   59
17. That Thing You Do   62
18. Yolo Legacy   65

19.	And Suddenly, You Are Home	68
20.	Simple Sustenance	71
21.	Ohana	76
22.	A Legacy of Love	79
23.	Michelangelic	83
24.	Lagom	86
25.	The Vagus Nerve	89
26.	The Quarantine of 2020	92

Epilogue — *95*

PROLOGUE

Like an adventurer who sets out with nothing but a thirst for travel, I embarked on an inward journey in 2014, that, moving forward, became more and more cathartic. My goal was to observe life, learn what it had to teach me, and, most importantly, 'just live it'. What resulted over the years is a life deliberately lived, held dear, and made simpler with every new lesson.

I believe that 'everyone comes from somewhere'. It is an idea that sustains me and gives me the courage to honour my worth, without which my words would never have found their way into the world. I can say with great conviction that our seemingly unadorned lives and modest legacies do matter in the greater scheme of things.

As you move from one narrative to the next, pause awhile and ponder. Appreciate your blessings, understand your struggles, and hold each precious moment with the utmost tenderness. Life is simple and spiritual. Let us experience it joyfully, one day at a time.

Renica Rego
January 2021, Mumbai

MISTY MEADOWS

As we drove higher and higher into the mountains, the mist got thicker. Visibility was limited to about three meters ahead. Quite suddenly, the rain started pelting down heavily, blinding us even more. The pounding of raindrops fused with Jamie Lawson crooning, *'I wasn't expecting that';* music within and without, with a similar cadence. It was the most surreal drive of my life. The road was narrow and steep and opened up dangerously to the valley on either side. All we had to lead us further was the faint blink of lights from the car ahead of us. That's exactly how the past few months had been; hazy and blatantly exigent.

At some point, though, the fog always clears. And so, finally, after an interminable wait, things had started falling into place. Life makes you wait, testing your patience, your faith, your strength. It makes you doubt everything that you thus far believed in. And then, suddenly, like a burst of unexpected rain, the abundance showers right down on your startled head.

We had left the city behind and were headed to the hills on an impulse. It was an impromptu plan and one that made me want to live the rest of my life in that manner – purely spontaneous and unpremeditated.

We arrived at 'Misty Meadows' just as dusk was settling in. A warm, welcoming glow radiated from idyllic houses that lined the streets. Life seemed tranquil and quiet on those moorlands. We spent that evening devoid of distractions. There was no Wi-Fi and no television, just words and smiles floating around. After a simple meal, we retired to the bedrooms upstairs. The river in the distance was beautiful in the twilight. We could spot cars parked on the bridge over the river, and made up stories about clandestine affairs and romantic conversations, giggling our way into the silly night.

The next morning, I woke up at dawn. It was still dark when I wandered onto the terrace, shivering slightly but warmed by the soothing silence. The moon was hanging in the sky like a neatly clipped fingernail, obscured now and then by the pregnant clouds. As I lingered, the sun came up unseen and the silhouette of the meadows appeared through the brooding mist.

It was after breakfast that we embarked upon that haunting drive. Later, as we stumbled upon rocks and puddles, walked on lush meadows, and gazed upon verdant hills, I realized how close we had come to God in those few hours. All my five senses seemed numbed, but there was a sixth sense that seemed sharper than the five put together. A divine presence was everywhere, in every detail. Half-encumbered in this realization, and sloshed by the weight I'd been carrying around, I plonked down on a rock. Fatigue mingled with raindrops and rolled down my back, leaving me cleansed and a little narcotized.

This whole experience was much like what the Japanese call '*Shinrin-yoku*' or 'Forest Bathing'. It was first proposed in 1982 by the Forest Agency of Japan, to promote a good lifestyle, and is now a recognized stress management activity in Japan. My fascination with the Japanese culture is now bordering on reverence, threatening to override my absolute fascination with the Tuscan way of life. It is strange because they seem absolutely converse. Tuscans are voluble while the Japanese are more muted; but if you make a reduction, the essence is the same: simplicity.

Growing up, I had the good fortune of experiencing '*Shinrin-yoku*' often. Hardened by city life, though, we become impertinent and that is why it is absolutely important to make an effort to get dwarfed by nature and humble ourselves from time to time. It is in such moments that we find clarity and direction. It is then that we are filled with hope. And, from nature, we learn one great lesson: to trust the timing of our life.

LOSING FINGERPRINTS

I was probably a third-grader when my first letter arrived in the mail. The fact that an envelope bore my name made me feel important, and the idea of someone writing to me was beyond magical.

That was the first of a series of letters that soon became my only hope of knowing a father who was physically absent from my young life. Dad had left for foreign shores when I was barely three. The only connection we could have, apart from his annual visits, was through those letters. They were beautifully written in a bold, cursive hand, and ran into multiple pages. The dreariness of many a sultry afternoon was thus made luminescent by the simple arrival of a letter.

A couple of years later, leafing through a magazine in the library, I came across the concept of 'pen friends'. It was a fascinating thought and I lost no time in subscribing to the 'Pen Pals Club'. We passionately wrote to each other across countries and continents, sharing our humdrum life that the other found suitably exotic. To our innocent minds, it was a delightful experience, as thrilling as physically discovering a new city.

It might seem strange that in an age of speedy digital communication, I'm longing for an era gone by. The virtual world is great and there is no end to how far one can go. But, for our own good, we need to rein ourselves in and know where to draw the line. Thanks to social media, we've initiated new relationships and rekindled old ones by the dozen. But how many of them have any depth? And where is the honesty in our altered, pseudo lives? While, seemingly, being in touch with a lot of people, we are drifting away from the ones around us and also our own selves. Is the endless typing making us lose our fingerprints?

In his book, *The Art of Stillness*, Pico Iyer writes: "The very people [...] who have worked to speed up the world are the same ones most sensitive to the virtue of slowing down." He goes on to describe his visit to the Google headquarters where he found "the workers at the time enjoying a fifth of their working hours free, letting their minds wander off-leash to where inspiration might be hiding." As they say in Kyoto, "Don't just do something. Sit there."

So, while I stay attuned to the times, I'd like to sporadically veer off towards old-fashioned ways. The onslaught of information and inane chats are jarring to the soul; making me long for calming voices and meaningful conversations over steaming cups of coffee in real cafés. It would be nice to look into people's eyes and hear their laughter instead of deciphering emoticons. It would be refreshing to hear people say words that they really, truly mean. Why can't we give and receive real flowers instead of virtual ones and, occasionally, go through the trouble of mailing a handwritten letter? At the risk of sounding passé, I crave the allure of things gone by.

Three days ago, it was my friend Marie's birth anniversary. The last time I saw her was half a decade ago. I remember our last meal together in Dubai when I told her that we were moving back to India; she had recoiled as if something had hit her. Saying a tearful goodbye, we had promised to write to each other, but sadly never did. Five years later, she was flown home and I was feeding her little morsels of bland rice in a dismal hospital room. The next day, she was gone. That image of her doesn't leave me. If only I had those letters we never wrote to each other!

As I lay half-awake the next morning, memories came to me like snippets of a strange dream. Later, I found myself on a park bench, pen poised over a notepad, starting a letter that I had promised a friend two months ago. I couldn't live with another broken promise. As if on cue, the pigeons settled around me like a clique. Sunshine filtered through the leaves. I recalled that the Japanese have a term for it: 'Komorebi', this interplay of light and leaves on the ground. There is a science behind it, but I couldn't be bothered right then. Just that it seemed beautifully premeditated and made for an aesthetically perfect setting.

A DELIBERATE LIFE

February had mostly been about silence, quietude, classified thoughts, and reclaiming personal time. I went back and forth into my shell, spoke less and read more. It felt good to not push the trite moments away while embracing the pristine. The in-between ones, I picked to refine the road maps to a life I never want to stop being in love with. Personal goals, however, seem fragmented if they don't cause at least a tiddly positive ripple that extends beyond our 'self'. As I went about setting intentions for the coming year, questions kept inadvertently popping up: "Do the benefits of a minimalist life extend to society?"; "How can I make a significant change?"; "What kind of trail am I leaving behind?" Regardless of who we are, each one of us has a wisdom that the world needs.

When I bid adieu to the corporate world, the first change was to draw a separation between the needs and wants. When you make a decision to go from clutching at bits of life in between the frenzy to enjoying a deliberate life, little alterations are necessary. In retrospect, that's when the shift had subtly begun. My daughter was five at the time, and her first lesson in 'enoughism' was to be mindful of what she picked up at the supermarket. We called it the 'one dirham' rule. If it cost one dirham or less, she could have it. When *Barbie* became a rage, she was encouraged to play with simpler, more wholesome-looking dolls. Without even realising it, the micro-decisions were adding up. Now, as an adult, when I see her spend wisely or choose character over status while picking friends, it seems like we did something right.

Minimalism is not about deprivation, you just need to know when to rein it in, and it's only human to slip sometimes. But we have to understand the consequences of our actions. The undercurrents of consumerism run deep. Like termites that stay hidden from sight until the rafters come crashing down, it eats away at the very fabric that is supposed to hold us together. How did we morph into a perpetually stressed lot, always running around, always distracted, and always in a quest to accumulate more? A bunch of robots so busy holding on to devices that we don't even realise what we have let go of? The litter we are leaving behind is worrisome. It's overwhelming when you think about making amends, but we can start small and still make a difference.

The other day, I asked my daughter what her dream home looked like. "A well-kept studio apartment," she said, matter-of-factly. It might sound strange but it's mighty sensible.

When we live in small uncluttered spaces, conserve energy, and buy less, what happens is this: we bring down the CO_2 levels generated by the burning of all the fuel needed, to power the making of crap that we don't really need. So, the simplest way to reduce our carbon footprint and add value is to change the way we live.

Recently, I dined at a new restaurant in my neighbourhood. It turned out to be a beautiful experience. The music was lilting, the staff friendly, the menu handpicked, and the food fresh. The server explained every dish to me right down to the sourcing of the ingredients. Their USP was 'fresh, organic, and simple'. That meal was poetry in motion and seemed like a perfect metaphor for the life I was aiming at.

One of life's simpler pleasures is always dessert. When the tiramisu came, the proprietor, a young man in his twenties, threw me a challenge. "Identify the five spices in this dessert and you get a parting drink on the house," he chimed. As I rolled a spoonful of the dessert on my tongue, the spices stood out enough for me to name them correctly. I got the free drink as promised. But the most valuable takeaway was this: whether it's food, possessions, or life, when you eliminate the superfluity, what remains is the essence.

THE IMPORTANCE OF BEING BEAUTIFUL

I was the "in full acne bloom" kind of teenager, who withdraws into layers and layers of shell. My flawed skin wasn't really the problem, the way people defined beauty was. But I was too young to realize that. It was uncaringly pointed out that my face was marred and my chances of landing a good husband were ruined. It was appalling! Little did they realize that their lack of empathy would disfigure me more than a skin blemish ever could. For a long time, my self-esteem remained fluid at best. As I grew older though, it became apparent that there were far more important things than worrying about a mere reflection in the mirror. This kind of realization is like the subtle shifting of tectonic plates that causes the earth to move. And move I did – from who I was expected to be, to who I inherently was.

Over the years, I have been fortunate to be blessed with people who never let me forget my worth. My daughter, Rhea, is one such person. She doesn't use words to express her love, but when she hugs, it's like the ardour of the love gods descending on you! She is, without a doubt, one of the most loving people I know. Recently, I received a book in the mail; a surprise gift from her. It was an adult colouring book, the kind used for meditative purposes. In choosing that gift, she had expressed so much. It was her way of sustaining my creativity, encouraging my growth, and, in the process, simply saying that I matter. To me, that kind of gesture is beauty in its most dazzling form.

In his book *Who Will Cry When You Die?*, Robin Sharma writes about creating a love account. He talks about how our random acts of kindness and selfless acts of beauty can make someone's day better. He urges us to practise being more loving by making a few deposits in this very special reserve by doing something small to add joy to the life of someone around us. A simple text message asking how someone's day was, sharing a favourite song, recounting an anecdote or episode, a warm hug, a small little surprise in the mail are little things that say 'you are loved and appreciated'. Making at least one person feel worthy should be our goal on any given day.

There's an interesting story about an African tribe. The identity of the tribe is debatable, but what fascinated me was the message. In this tribe, whenever a person misbehaves, he is summoned to the centre of the village. Everyone gathers around him in a circle. Then, one by one, each person present speaks to him about all the good he has done in the past. They talk about his strengths, kindness, and virtues. This ceremony stems from the belief that we are all essentially good, but sometimes we make mistakes. The tribe sees those mistakes as a cry for help. By reminding him of all his goodness, they reconnect him to his true, pure self. How beautiful it is that someone reminds you of your wholeness when you're broken; your beauty when you feel ugly.

One particularly enlightening lesson came to me from a friend about the *'kasturi-mriga'* or musk deer. When this particular deer catches wind of the alluring aroma of musk, he rambles on in pursuit of its source. The poor soul doesn't realize that the sweet fragrance resides in its own navel. We are quite often like the *'kasturi-mriga'*, searching 'without' for what is, all along, lying 'within'.

As I open myself up to life, the meanings and lessons become more discernible. My favourite realisation is that there is so much yet to learn. But some things I am certain of. I am clear about my idea of beauty and it is certainly not about how you look. It is about courage and smiling through tears. It is about being there for someone who needs you, listening to a friend who is pouring their heart out even if you yourself are broken, making people feel like they are not alone. Kindness is beautiful. Love and empathy are beautiful. Being authentic is beautiful. Unfolding and evolving is beautiful.

WANDER MORE OFTEN

When we first arrived at my aunt's place on B.C. Road, it was a clear, sunlit morning. As we wandered around the grounds, I marvelled at how verdant it all looked. Rows of swaying coconut palms, mangoes dangling from overburdened trees, the nonchalantly masticating cows, the raucous cackling of the chickens; it was all very nice. But, for me, the real fascination came after dusk. Life stilled to a whisper, except for the chirping of the nocturnal crickets and the warm glow of fireflies. I perched myself on the low wall that marked the boundary, just sitting there in the twilight, one with the magnetic silence. It is only when a panicked search party came looking for me that I realized I'd been sitting there for over an hour. It was an allegorical night and, later in bed, I remember jotting down three words in my journal: *Wander more often*. I was fourteen then.

Recently, reading a piece on spin tops triggered the above memory. I've always been fascinated by this humble toy but never been good at actually making one spin. But now, I started thinking about the mechanics of it: the way it spins and the motion which causes it to remain perfectly balanced on its tip because of inertia. The balanced languor of that inert night, in an otherwise rapidly spinning world, was quite akin to the spin-top theory.

When my yoga teacher taught me meditation a few years ago, this is what he had said: "Relax and breathe. Watch your thoughts as they come, and let them go. Be the passive outsider. Eventually, you will reach a point of total clarity. That's when you will feel awake." In the words of Jigar Gor, "Yoga is not about touching your toes, it is what you learn on the way down." This is exactly what my guru was trying to teach me. Clearly, 'awakening' is not limited to ten minutes in a lotus position. You come to your yoga mat to feel, not to accomplish. His words resound in my mind now with a fortified meaning. Meaning that extends to all of life. Some nights, lying awake in bed, thinking, I realize that somewhere along the way, I seemed to have relinquished all that I'd learnt. Balance begs to be restored. Lost ideas float around like confetti in the brain. These aren't delusions of an insomniac mind but colossal blunders that need to be dealt with.

Like any child, while growing up I've had my moments of open-mouthed wonder. One such event was a magic show I attended. Gaping at the magician's every trick, I was drawn into a kind of parallel universe. It was like moving in and out of real and magical worlds all at once. The experience was beyond anything I'd experienced thus far. The witnessing of such a feat was, to me, nothing short of a gift. But the actual gift was hidden, lost in translation, and too nebulous for an infantile mind to comprehend. I've tried a lot of stuff since but it's only now, well into my fourth decade, that I grasped the full meaning of an idea that was simple enough to be radical.

All the yoga and meditation had so far come to nought just because I had missed one little point – *unmitigated letting go*. I had assumed that my guru wanted me to let go of the negative thoughts, but now I realized that he hadn't really specified that.

Our minds, and thus our lives, are like that magic show. It is all about perception. What we believe becomes real. Quite suddenly, 'being in the moment' took on a new meaning. It takes a bit of effort and courage to peel away the layers that have gathered over time. And unless you're Archimedes, it's certainly never a mind-blowing eureka moment in a bathtub when you finally discover what really works. It's an uphill climb with constant landslides that hurl you back to where you began.

As is slowly becoming evident, I'm certainly not as Utopian as my poetic temperament indicates. When there is an inherent need to put every idea into practice and make it work, the flotsam of idealism ploddingly gives way to sparkling reality. The mental back and forth, the search for experiences, the spiritual connections, the craving to taste life turns one into a nomad without ever travelling much. You grow adept at ruminating with your eyes wide open. Not unlike the cow in my aunt's barn who chewed on its cud all day long, the crunch of impassioned musings keeps me going most times.

As I grow older, the physical journey moves in tandem with the spiritual one. Regardless of the maturity that comes in spurts, life doesn't cease to be ambivalent. Even then, with each passing year, I come closer to my inner nomad. And, for that, I am eternally grateful. The lack of ostentation in a nomadic life appeals to me. For a nomad, even a stationary one, the truth is not really in the wandering, it is in the 'unmitigated letting go'.

THE LIGHTHOUSE

Mum, Dad, and I sat on the stone bench watching waves scatter themselves on the rocks. The tide was high and, in the distance, a few boats dotted the ocean. To our right, the lighthouse of Kapu stood tall and majestic against the sky. I was drawn to its beauty, the way it portrayed grace and strength. Mum was narrating some anecdote, as usual, the strong wind making her voice fade now and then. Dragging my eyes away from the lighthouse, I focused on her. A no-precept kind of woman, who rarely preaches, she has always believed in lovingly doing what needs to be done. What can be more exemplary than a compassionate and righteous person, I thought.

My parents had recently moved from Mumbai to Udupi and I was visiting them. Our five days together only augmented how terribly I missed them. It also made me think a lot about the role of parents, how much indirect influences matter, and the myopic attitude we have towards our own kids, the so-called millennials and post-millennials.

Consider for a moment the little things you do as a parent. Do you just preach or do you lead by example?

Do you remember and live by the values your parents taught you? Think about your childhood days, when family and friends just dropped in without intimation. Reflect on how your parents welcomed them with so much warmth, making sure they were fed with whatever little was available while enjoying genuine conversations. How involved family, neighbours, and friends were in each other's lives!

Our home was small but it was always filled with people. When guests stayed the night, we happily offered them our bed and slept dorm-style on floor-mats covered with thin quilts. When an uncle or aunt reprimanded us, neither we nor our parents took offence. Now, when we bump into someone, we half-heartedly say, "Hey, it's been long. Drop-in sometime. *But please call before you come.*" If a family member drops in without intimation, we don't like it.

The first thing we need to do is throw open our hearts and doors. Growing up in a *chawl*, the only time we used to shut our doors was at bedtime. We walked into neighbour's houses and ate from their pots without inhibition. We visited our family regularly, spent summers at an aunt's or grandparent's place, went on Sunday picnics, and lived as humans should. When did we become islands? What happened to us? Where did the community spirit go?

I once read an article about how during the '*wintering in*' period in places like Antarctica, it has been observed how much isolation affects a human being. Appetite, sleep patterns, ability to concentrate, etc. are greatly affected. Boredom from being around the same people leads to annoyance and dislike. Is this why we have compromised immune systems or continue to suffer from early cognitive decline? Have you ever thought about the perils of social isolation and how we have shaped a generation that is completely *shut-in*?

On my return flight, as the aeroplane bounced around on the iridescent clouds, the turbulence reminded me of the lighthouse. How it never moves or jumps into the unruly ocean to rescue floundering ships, but stands quiet and firm, its beacon casting light so the mariners can find their own way to safety. I thought of mum saying goodbye with a trembling smile, her small frame lost in my embrace, and realized how akin to a lighthouse she was. Was I taking her legacy forward? Was I being a good parent? Before I found fault with my daughter, was I willing to point a finger at my own self?

It is rightly said that children come through us, not from us, and all we need to do is set a good example. My dignity as a parent lay in standing firm and strong, upholding values, and just being a guiding light when required, much like the lighthouse.

Life for our children can sometimes get more turbulent than they can handle. In the words of M. L. Stedman, "There are times when the ocean is not the ocean – not blue, not even water, but some violent explosion of energy and danger: ferocity on a scale only gods can summon. It hurls itself at the island, sending spray right over the top of the lighthouse, biting pieces off the cliff. And the sound is a roaring of a beast whose anger knows no limits. Those are the nights the light is needed the most."

SAVED BY A SONG

It was one of those rare occasions when I had wandered into a church. As my knees hit the floor, the strains of 'Old Rugged Cross' filled the air; hundreds of voices rose in crescendo and tears came rolling down. After two years of my friend Marie's passing, the floodgates had finally opened. That celestial moment became my testament to the undeniable healing power of music.

Being a loner all through my teen years, the only true connection I had was with music and words. On long afternoons, I was almost always found huddled in a corner with a book, and, in the evenings, with my tiny music player in a dimly-lit room. Music has been a constant, but the bedtime tradition that had waned over time is now revived and made sacred. Once I'm alone in my room, the windows are thrown open and the music comes in. Embellished by moonlight and kissed by the gentle breeze, the sounds seem ethereal. It is, without a doubt, the most magical part of my day.

Years ago, when I had signed up for piano classes, my music teacher had encouraged me to look for life lessons in music. "If you let it all the way in, music can bring about a real catharsis," she had said. It's true. Music can foster unity with another mind, another culture, and life itself, giving us insight like nothing else can. On some days it is jazz, on other days rock, or sometimes a forgotten Bollywood classic. The music we play is never random; either we choose it or it chooses us. That's exactly why we get obsessed with certain songs; it's because they speak to our deeper selves.

I have an inherent need to understand a song in all its entirety. So, recently, when a friend sent me a Bangla song, it upset me that I couldn't find a proper translation of the lyrics. "You would have enjoyed it more," he said wryly, "if you just *listened* to it." That, right there, was another analogy for life.

The struggle to find our worth can be an ongoing battle. A broken relationship, an unfulfilling career, or a lost dream can leave us feeling shoddy. Until one day, someone holds a mirror to our soul and we remember love. Just like the beauty of a person is revealed by how they make you feel, so it is with music. A song that you find mediocre could be someone's favourite just because it spoke to them when they needed it the most. It's a thought that has made me more accepting of other people's choices, in music and in life.

Whether it's a long journey or a dark patch I'm trying to work through, what has, and always will help me, is a piece of music. Above all else, it teaches us that love is more than just a word. It's our connection with the world around us. It helps us make sense of the chaos that surrounds us. It shows us that no matter where we live on this planet, we are essentially the same. Sometimes, when I find myself withering, I sit back and let a song wash over me; at other times, I write my own. Either way, it can be safely said that I'm always saved by a song. A single lyric or melody at the right time can change everything. It can give you direction, beauty, meaning, and the courage to live with a little more heart.

There's a quote from *One Tree Hill* that I love. "Every song has a coda, a final movement. Whether it fades out or crashes away, every song ends. Is that any reason not to enjoy the music?" We're all perpetually trying to figure things out, working our way through the rough terrain of life, wondering where it leads us. Well, with the right soundtrack, our journey can be a transcendent one.

LIKE A LOTUS LEAF

Back in middle school, I was once summoned to Fr. Dennis' office. He was my teacher, confidant, and guide, all rolled into one. I was a painfully shy kid, but Fr. Dennis knew how to draw me out. That morning, he handed me the Bible, asked me to pick a passage and read it aloud. I meekly obeyed not knowing what was in store for me. When I finished, he smiled and said, "You read well and have a beautiful voice. This Sunday you will do the First Reading during the children's service." I stood rooted to the spot. I couldn't do it! I had stage fright! But all my protests fell on deaf ears.

That particular Sunday came all too soon and I found myself standing on the dais, the Bible in my hand, my voice surprisingly clear and strong enough to reach the farthermost members of the congregation. It was one of those small yet defining moments; the kind where you realize that you're capable of more than what you give yourself credit for. My life, up until then, had been covered with a veil of ambiguity. But little revelations like these gradually spurred an inward journey.

During our formative years, we are taught a lot of things, but no one teaches us how to love and espouse ourselves. In addition to the indiscriminate syllabus at school, we are conditioned by society to worry about what others think, to downplay our talents, to belittle our accomplishments and compromise on our dreams. It is no wonder then that along the way, we lose our light and purpose. We lead a life set on autopilot, designed by choices that, more often than not, are directly or discreetly made for us by someone else.

In the late 1990s, as part of my creative writing course, my mentor assigned me a project. I had to pick a topic, interview a few people, and present a paper worthy of his perusal. The title on my assignment read: ARE YOU LIVING YOUR BEST LIFE? It was disconcerting to find that most people I interviewed weren't happy. They regretted giving up on their dreams and longed for a more vibrant life. When they spoke about their passions, their eyes lit up and their faces took on a glow. At that moment, they seemed to radiate their true selves. It is never too late though, no matter how old we are. This is the kind of intention we must release into the Universe: TO LIVE OUR BEST LIVES. It might sound grand but it is actually pretty basic.

There is a majestic looking 'Global Vipassana Pagoda', a Buddhist meditation hall near Gorai, Mumbai, not too far from where I live. I love going there as often as possible. The pagoda itself, built on a peninsula between the Gorai creek and the Arabian Sea, is beautiful and there is a serenity that covers the place like a precious blanket. But I'm always drawn to the fringes, to what is around the central theme, be it a place or a person. The first time I went there, my exploration of the grounds led me to a lovely lotus pond. It is a 'ruminations' kind of place, where you lose track of time.

On the ferry ride back, my thoughts kept drifting to the lotus pond; more specifically, the lotus leaves. These leaves have a unique feature. They are 'super-hydrophobic', meaning that their surface is extremely difficult to wet. Because of this, the lotus flower can thrive in the muddiest of lakes or the dirtiest of ponds without getting affected. All because the water rolls right off the leaves that surround and protect the flower. Shouldn't this be exactly how we mould ourselves? By remaining connected to our 'selves' and letting all that negates our progress 'roll off', we might be able to stay true to our path, no matter where we are at right now.

As the old year folded into the new, I took a wander in the labyrinth of my mind. There is always so much going on there that it's hard to discern and sift the marginal from the crucial. I sat, watching the setting sun, the air smelling of burnt wood drifting from afar. And just when a perfectly quiet moment, bereft of clutter, came along, I made a simple and mindful intent: EMULATE A LOTUS LEAF. To a spirit like mine that gets easily jaded, it might be a Herculean enterprise, but I'm willing to try. As my Reiki Master always said, "Intention is everything."

THE SILENCE BETWEEN

It was the Zen-blue sky that hit me first. As I taxied out into the city, my skin absorbing the cool breeze like water on parched soil, Bengaluru appeared to be welcoming me. For some strange reason, it felt like grandpa's wrinkled arms and toothless grin beckoning me home. Quite enamoured, I walked into my husband's Marathahalli apartment, with an uncanny feeling that the following week was about to change something in me.

The next six days were spent wandering around, exploring the city. No place is, as such, perfect to its residents. Anyone who lives in Bengaluru will most definitely complain about the traffic that seems lodged on flyovers and in narrow lanes likes clinging parasites. But, as an outsider, I subliminally saw something significant that alleviated the burden of it for me. By the evening of the first day itself, I had discounted all the snags in favour of the one thing that stood out in the locals of this ordinary city. And that was their unruffled serenity. There was a sense of collective calm despite the bustle. People chatted amicably with strangers in buses and auto-rickshaw drivers grinned charmingly while demanding ridiculous fares. When a car hit our taxi at a signal, the cabbie got out, inspected the damage, shook his head slightly, 'paused' for a second, and then waved it off. No anger, no foul language. That is probably the key to composure – the pause. Mozart, the prolific composer of the classical era believed that "the music is not in the notes, but in the silence between." Maybe that is how our mind should function too. I found myself inspecting the connotations, reading the sub-text, and collecting wistful images to carry home.

On day two, sauntering through the Lalbaug Botanical Gardens, I came across a colourful statue of Nandi. Typically, Nandi being Lord Shiva's vehicle, is always found sitting at the doorway of the temple in a perpetually silent but alert waiting mode. Nandi, thus, has gained on a symbolism, teaching us the virtue of simply sitting, vigilant but without expectations. The image of Nandi essentially reminds us to pause and pay attention to life. Only in the pauses can the music of the Universe be heard.

The next day, my friend Suzanne invited me to lunch. After a sumptuous meal, she and I set out for a stroll by the Ulsoor lake, not far from her home. As was wont to happen, we delved into a deep conversation. "There's a reason we feel so calm and alive being around nature," she remarked touching the leaves that hung over our bench and gazing at the serene lake. "It's because nature never pretends to be what it's not. A leaf is a leaf, content and happy with its true form. That's why we feel good around people who are like that too."

As I mulled over this, it became apparent why I had thought of grandpa the day I arrived. Grandpa was like that, content and cheerful, demanding nothing from life and never pretending to be what he's not. He would gallivant, stop to chat with everyone on the street, lose track of time, and come home with the fading sun, bringing a sack of fish. Grandma would get livid and hurl the sack in the fire, but grandpa only laughed. "Why are you so angry, Eliza?" he would ask, nudging her playfully. It was the same kind of simplicity that I now saw in the locals of Bangalore.

As my week drew to an end, I found myself feeling grateful for the pauses that presented themselves from time to time. Devoid of distractions, the subtle joy of such experiences steadily engages and unfills me, at the same time. As I prepared to leave, the sky that I had so fallen in love with became even more luminous, as if allowing me one more image to colour my reminiscences with.

Back home in Mumbai, days eased by in one uninterrupted flow. The rain was pelting down in bursts, bringing a refreshed brilliance to the days, and the nights were made snug by the warmth of fluffy blankets. Everything seemed revived by the clarity I had acquired from my time away.

One afternoon, that same week, I came across a classic Zen story narrated by Zen master Fukushimaroshi to the acclaimed writer, Pico Iyer. One day, an old man was trying to explain to his grandchild about Jōdo Buddhism, and he said, "In the West — that's where the pure land is!" And the child pointed out that if you go west and west, you go right around the world, and come back round to where you are!

TABLE FOR ONE

If I remember right, it was in class 8th that we were asked to analyze William Wordsworth's lyrical poem, 'I wandered lonely as a cloud' (more popularly known as 'Daffodils'). Being a loner at heart, and often indulging in such wanderings myself, I found it easy to relate to this simple yet profound piece of work. My English teacher had applauded it as a sincere and well-comprehended analysis. Having recently lost his brother, Wordsworth was actually melancholic at the time he wrote the poem, but I knew my own wanderings were not really dismal. 'Being alone' did not have to mean 'being lonely'.

Years later, life nudged me to revisit the cognizance of the 12-year-old me. Every decade of life brings new learning, but the forties have been really profound. After over two decades of constantly hovering around each other, my husband had to, without much notice, move to Bangalore for work. It brought back solitude in heaps, the minutes piling up like an untidy collection of objects placed haphazardly on top of each other. At first, it was overwhelming, but, in due course, the aesthete in me started coherently stacking up the hours in neat, codified piles. It was an opportunity to feed the 'slow life' fanatic in me and before I knew it, I was addicted to the unceremoniously strewn moments.

Women raised in patriarchal societies are conditioned to calibrate from a young age and that kind of encumbrance eventually becomes a roadblock that we subconsciously set up for ourselves. We grow up believing that it is somehow wrong to enjoy a movie on our own or go out with friends if the husband and kids are at home. So, one fine day, when solitude comes knocking, we don't know what to do.

Many years ago, during my junior college days, I had to appear for an exam. Having reached the examination centre too early, I decided to grab a sandwich at a nearby restaurant to kill time. It did not occur to me that sitting by myself in a restaurant was such a big deal, but clearly, it was. I was catcalled and stared at. It was mortifying and the incident made me guarded and even more diffident than I already was.

Things are, thankfully, different now. I recently read that 'good at being alone' is seen as a skill important enough to be put on a resume in countries like Japan. The late Japanese journalist Iwashita Kumiko, in 1999, coined an interesting term called *O-hitori Sama Kojo Iinkai* (the committee for advancing the interests of people who do things alone). *O-hitori sama*, more than anything else, has become a newly coined expression to describe women soloing out, and I am heartened to see that the trend is catching up in Indian cities too. When I now enter a restaurant, after a solo shopping trip, it seems unremarkable to say, "Table for one, please." On a deeper level, it is quantum leaps such as these that transform society from the ground up. As individuals, it sets us free.

I'm not really a 'spa person', but after a particularly disorienting day, walking the bylanes of Pratunam in Thailand, I once allowed myself to be coaxed into a foot massage. As the masseuse worked deftly to un-knot my muscles, I eased into a trance and, an hour later, emerged out of there thoroughly rejuvenated. Solitude is much like that. There's something profound about being alone and I am beginning to relish the beauty of it.

Humans are social animals and company is always welcome. So, in essence, I am by no means promoting *soloism* (if there is such a term), but am just upholding the merits of such a state if you ever find yourself in it. These are the fringe benefits of a situation that most people consider sombre. The "bliss of solitude" as Wordsworth put it, is worth exploring. Life is so interesting and vast that time falls short. So, it's prudent to not waste time waiting for company when there is none, but rather to go after what ignites us and sets our hearts aflutter. And, while we're at it, let's not forget that there are lessons to be learned and thoughts to be shared. If while 'wandering lonely as a cloud' we can unleash our creativity, share and inspire someone with our experiences, then we can leave knowing that we honoured the magnanimous gift of life.

INTO THE FOREST

Last week, we drove down to Atvan for a much-needed getaway. The morning was beautifully cleansed by a steady drizzle and soulful music filled the air. As we drove higher up on the hill, the slow upward climb was made surreal by the dense fog that hung over the valley like a thick, fluffy blanket.

Atvan in Marathi means 'into the forest'. After a short, rickety ride off the main road, we came upon the iron gates of the property where we were to spend the next couple of days. It was like stepping into another world, where all one could do was just 'be'. The foliage was thick and lustrous, the skies weeping in bursts every now and then. A subtle peace hung in the air and clung to us as we walked down the suspended wooden bridge that led to our treehouse. It felt like ambling through a paradise that promised to hold and nurture me.

The treehouse itself was splendid. The lines between the indoors and outdoors were so artfully blurred that I could reach out over the balcony and touch the branches. The best thing, however, was the birdsong. For the first time, I discovered the salacious warbling of the

'Malabar Whistling Thrush', aptly nicknamed 'Whistling Schoolboy'. The call of this bird has an uncannily human quality about it and the constant trill kept me amused throughout my stay there.

While there was still light, we explored the forest, walking along winding pathways and climbing slippery slopes. There were very few people around and it was just as well. The quietude was welcome and calmed my heart like nothing else could. It was very reminiscent of my summers in pre-electric Mangalore when the only illumination after dusk came from small lamps scattered around the house. Oftentimes, I long for those inky nights that were spent gazing at radiantly starry skies.

Mostly, I am a happy person, but I suffer from intermittent existential malaise. There is a melancholy that runs through my veins, and, most times, that very darkness seems to inspire my creativity. Of late though, there had been constant spells of anxiety that rattled and numbed me in cycles. It wasn't a good feeling. But, right then, in the lap of nature, it seemed possible to wipe away the grime, lay down for a bit, and stand up again. I felt ready to re-focus and re-calibrate. That said, the learning curve was yet to present itself.

As the day folded into the night, a swarm of moths came out. The night was punctuated with their calls, but other than that it was a world that demanded nothing. As I snuggled under the covers, peering out into the night through the glass wall, a stellar spectacle built up before me. With wide-eyed wonder, I witnessed the effervescent dance of hundreds of glowing fireflies. It was like a secret performance planned just for me. So dazzled was I, that it kept me awake for hours watching as they twinkled and dimmed until I could no longer tell them apart from the stars above.

The bioluminescence of a firefly is an enchanting process that involves the conversion of chemical energy into light. Could these little beacons of hope then be passing on a lesson? That no matter how much darkness we're drenched in, we could radiate our own light? Lost in the embrace of that soft, mesmeric night, I surrendered to the alluring flashes of life that these little critters brought me. For, as they say, every blink of a firefly's light says 'believe'.

THE SILVER OAK

The minute I stepped out of Cochin International Airport, I intuitively knew that this was a place that would resonate with my soul. Mr Sudhan, our driver and guide, promptly arrived with a wide smile, his appearance as immaculate as the silver sedan he drove. Little did I know then that this man would soon charm his way into our hearts. A walking encyclopedia of not just the history and geography of Kerala, but any other topic under the sun. By the time we reached Munnar, five hours later, he had become my Sudhan *cheta*, meaning "brother" in Malayalam.

On the way, he pointed out Adi Shankaracharya's Keerthi stambha, Kalady, the Periyar river, and briefly let us out at the Cheeyapara waterfalls. As I stretched my tired back, he handed me a small lime and said, "Madam, scratch the skin and inhale. Zig-zag road ahead. Good for nausea." When it was time for lunch, we were desperate for the famous beef roast and Malabar parottas, but *cheta* politely pointed out that we must stick to light, vegetarian food as our bodies were tired and the road ahead was bad. I was charmed.

The next morning, we headed for the Devikulam tea gardens. The small village of Devikulam nestles amidst verdant green slopes, the clouds hanging low on the colourful houses, and a lovely chill enveloping the entire hill station. On the way, Sudhan *cheta* started playing some Hindi music to which I strongly protested. "Only Malayalam and Tamil music please,*cheta*," I requested. His face lit up and from there on, all the way to the Flower Garden and later the Lockhart Tea Museum, the discussion turned to our favourite music maestros, Illayaraja, Yesudas, SPB, Janaki, etc. He knew so much about music and movies that it stumped me. At the Lockhart Museum, we learnt a lot about tea, but, for me, music remained the highlight of that afternoon.

Later, walking down the Mattupetty bridge in the light drizzle, I met an old woman selling peanuts and fruits. She kept urging me to buy something. "My wallet is in the car, Amma," I said. She smiled fondly, forced a pack of peanuts in my hand, and replied in halting English, "You eat. Money later."

On the first day, Sudhan *cheta* had told us that Kerala produces twenty varieties of bananas and that every day he would have us taste a couple of them. As he dropped us back to the hotel, he handed us a packet and grinned, "Today, special red bananas."

The most scenic and beautiful sight was to unfold the following day. Refreshed from a good night's sleep, we enjoyed the light drizzle on the way to the Ernavikulam

National Park. Munnar is full of tea plantations, but the ride through this one, on the way to Rajamala Hills, was the most dramatic. As we stepped out at the foot of the hills, the rain stopped as if on cue. The uphill ramble, with the mountains towering on one side and the valley on the other, was the most beautiful walk I've ever been on. When we stopped mid-way, the view took my breath away. 'This is what paradise must look like,' I thought.

The fourth day we drove into a dream called Thekkady. With the quaint Periyar river, the sleepy beauty of the savanna grasslands, the thick deciduous forests, and the abundant wildlife, it was the perfect place for a nature lover like me.

After wafting for a couple of hours on the glassy river, we went on a spice trail. Our guide, Ms Sheeba, instantly won us over with her knowledge, heavily-accented Hindi, and a beautiful smile. By the end of the hour-long tour, we had more information about spices and herbs than our little brains could possibly hold. As we said our goodbyes to Sheeba, she scribbled her name on the brochure and said, "I wrote my name so you'll always remember me. I enjoyed talking to you because very few people show genuine interest like you did. Come back soon." At our resort, there was another spice whiz called Leeba. She took me around the huge estate, pointing at shrubs and trees, rattling off information and generally making a quick entry into my heart. Leeba means "love" and it was the perfect name for her.

There was more to unassuming Thekkady. That evening we found ourselves in a small, modest theatre watching Kathakali, one of the oldest theatre forms in the world. The performers were excellent with their expressions, *mudras,* and a short mythological presentation. That was followed by Kalaripayattu, a 3000-year old martial arts form, the oldest in the world. We had been tired that day and had meant to skip these shows, but Sudhan *cheta* insisted on taking us there. Any other man would have enjoyed the free evening, but he was clearly different. That night, I ate little for I was too full of nature, art, and love.

With much reluctance, we left Thekkady two days later, to spend the last day in Alleppy. "*Cheta*, I am in the land of coconuts, and you haven't treated me to coconut water yet," I playfully chided. He grinned and nodded. Driving past several tender coconut stalls, he stopped at one. "Only Kerala coconut for you, madam. Best coconut. You'll know when you taste it," he boasted. True to his word, the sweet taste of that water was an elixir to my parched throat.

The main attraction of Alleppy is, of course, boat rides on the backwaters. I enjoyed the ride, but the real highlight was meeting my Ayurvedic doctor, who I'd only communicated with on the phone for the past four years. The graciousness and love he and his family bestowed on us were heart-warming. On the way back, we asked Sudhan *cheta* how he knew even the by-lanes so well, without once using GPS. "GPS in my head, madam," he giggled.

"One last gift from me pending, madam," *cheta* crooned on the way to the airport the next morning. As he made a quick left turn from the highway, the magnificence of St. George's church left me gaping! It was by far the most beautiful church I had ever seen. Going down on my knees, I offered my gratitude for all the beauty and love that had come my way in that past week. From all the information Sudhan *cheta* had shared, one thing came back to me at that moment. Driving through the tree plantations, he had pointed to the tall trees that stood out awkwardly among the neatly trimmed tea plants. "Those silver oaks are planted on purpose, madam. Their roots go deep, hold the soil together, and help maintain moisture and nutrients. They also provide necessary shade for the tea plants. Basically, the tea plants flourish thanks to the silver oak."

Kerala is called 'God's Own Country', and every place we went to was bathed in pristine beauty and a natural sanctity that made it feel more like a pilgrimage than a holiday. But what has stayed with me is the memory of some wonderful people who, like silver oaks, held my ground with the warmth of their love, compassion, and humour.

A CASE FOR LOVE

February arrived like a co-conspirator of romance. It's a refreshing month that softens the soreness of splintered January resolutions. This year, the flirtatious Mumbai winter added to the mushiness. Interestingly, when it comes to romance, I've been intrigued by my own paradoxical behaviour. I write dreamy poetry but ask me to define love and I'm suddenly lost for words. With so many dimensions to it, it's an emotion that's hard to capture in a mere sentence.

Let's begin with the wider picture. Just last week, Pope Francis became the first pontiff to visit the Arabian peninsula. The visit was in conjunction with UAE's celebration of the Year of Tolerance, as declared by H. H. Sheikh Khalifa bin Zayed Al Nahyan, president of the UAE. Members of my family were fortunate enough to attend the ceremony and receive his blessings in person. What stood out for me though, was the deference and liberalism displayed by the hosts. Having lived in the UAE for over a decade, I can vouch for the open-mindedness of the rulers of this beautiful country. While religious strife continues to tear apart humanity, such gestures of acceptance underline the basis of love as taught by every religion known to mankind. This is a facet of love that needs urgent resurrection in these troubled times.

There is a beautiful motto: 'Love for All, Hatred for None' coined by the third spiritual leader of the Ahmadiyya Muslim Community, Hazrat Mirza Nasir Ahmad. Like Pope Francis, he upholds humility as the key quality that can ensure mutual love. He explains how Islam means 'peace' and it is only with mutual love and understanding that its principles can be upheld.

We all hanker for peace and harmony, but are we adding to the mayhem without even realizing it? Stop for a minute and think of all the data you've shared and received on social media. Add to that the drawing-room debates and chat room arguments. Think about how your direct or indirect participation can cause ripples that have far-reaching consequences. 'Thoughts become things', it's true. Why not stop re-hashing the same stories of dirty politics or religious disparities and focus on how we, as individuals, can make a difference? Why not direct our energy to the people around us? Do we even know what is going on in our own homes? Do we have the inclination to have real and meaningful conversations with our spouses, our children, our parents, our neighbours, our friends? Personal love extends to universal love; that's the connection I'm trying to make.

My daughter often laments that her generation has become so commitment-phobic that it's difficult to find someone you can trust. Why have people developed a fear for a simple and beautiful emotion like love? It's true that real love needs courage; it needs us to go past our egos and open our hearts. It involves caring, consideration, passion, and investment. Is that so difficult? Does the need for detachment come from fear and resistance? Where does this fear come from? We, as humans, are meant to love; it is a natural response of the heart. And love only gets bigger as we spread it around.

It is the eve of Valentine's Day, and as I look out at the fiery resplendence of the evening sky, I realize how love sets us on fire, filling us with a rare radiance. How when love is allowed to respond to life freely, it becomes miraculous. As we celebrate love tonight, let's pledge to honour and value what we have. World peace might sound ambitious, but once we learn to radiate the feeling to all, the celebration of love need not remain confined to a designated day. Happy love days ahead to all.

YUGEN

Strangely enough, on Christmas Day, I found myself on an inter-state train journey. The gradually changing landscape seemed metaphorical, reflecting the hazy passage of months gone by. Memories and thoughts bounced around in my head, keeping me awake through the 13-hour journey. Thankfully, my fellow passengers were a merry lot. They chatted with me, shared food, laughed, and felt like family. As they say, anything is possible on a train journey.

As everyone settled in for a snooze, I stood leaning against the doorway, basking in the soft rays of the setting sun. It felt like a '*kairos*' moment; the perfect time to let go of all the accumulated heaviness of the past year. In classical rhetoric, '*kairos*' refers to a proper or opportune time for action. As the train chugged along, I felt ready to get back on track.

The next morning, as I stepped out onto the red soil of my native land, there was a lightness in my step that had been missing for a while. Despite the unexpected heat, everything seemed to spark indescribable joy. The Japanese call it '*Yugen*', a profound awareness of the universe that triggers feelings too deep and mysterious for words to express. It is this very awareness that can supposedly turn our life around.

When he was little, my nephew sometimes would go and sit in the bathroom by himself. When asked why, he would sheepishly say, "I made a mistake, so I'm grounding myself." It was endearing and amusing at the same time. Grounding, unlike physical punishment, is a more positive corrective action. By taking away freedom or privileges, children are essentially taught to understand the consequences of their actions.

As adults, we need grounding too; a different kind, but a lot more restorative. The earth is a huge battery that contains natural electric charge. For safety and stability, almost everything in the electrical world is connected to it, whether it is an electric power plant or your refrigerator. That's what the term 'grounded' means, also known as 'earthing'. The same applies to us, too.

We are bio-electrical beings, but thanks to modern city life, we become so disconnected with the earth that it is inevitable that we feel a depletion of energy. Reconnecting is the only way we can charge our human batteries and remain healthy. Walking barefoot on a sandy beach or a stroll through the park is sufficient, to begin with. The countryside, for me, became the right place to initiate this kind of rejuvenation.

On one of my recent jaunts through the national park in my vicinity, I chanced upon the oldest tree there.

Just touching that beautiful tree trunk uplifted me. How mightily it had stood the test of time, through rainstorms and harsh winds! That should be our goal. To stay strong, majestic, and beautiful as we brave everything that life throws at us.

Whatever else you may have planned for the days ahead, remember to experience '*Yugen*' when possible, 'ground' yourself and stay vibrant. Keep bringing yourself back to the awareness from time to time. Do it often, and remind yourself that all of your power is in your awareness.

Michael Bernard Beckwith sums up the awareness of this power when he says, "Remember to remember!" Make this your theme. Here's to sparkling days ahead!

WABI SABI LIFE

Mrs Iyer and I met quite by chance. Her weathered face and kind eyes drew me towards her right away. There was something about this elderly woman that charmed me. It was the summer of 1999; a despondent phase which had taken me to a new low.

People who know me are familiar with my largely erratic memory. It is as if my neurons possess some sort of psychedelic sense of humour. Large chunks of data go missing without notice, and I can never recall things in tandem, but I do have visions from the past that are clear as if they happened yesterday. That is how I recall my time with Mrs Iyer, whom I eventually started calling *paati*, meaning grandmother in Tamil.

A few months after our first meeting, I quit my job, thus freeing up my evenings, many of which I chose to spend with *paati*. I had friends my age, but time with her somehow seemed sacred. *Paati* had a lot to share about her animated life with her husband, their travels together, and her recent loneliness after his demise. She was like a treasured book that I wished would never end. Our conversations spanned entire lifetimes, delved deep, and coloured our senses, mirroring the purple-orange sunsets of the Middle-Eastern skies. Our silhouettes in the fading light must have looked weird and wonderful at the same time; a fusing together of the old and the new. *Paati* taught me about impermanence, imperfection, and how to accept bits of our lives that remain unfinished. Above all, she taught me to embrace my flaws and appreciate myself.

In traditional Japanese aesthetics, *wabi-sabi* is a philosophy based on the acceptance of transience and imperfection. It is about embracing the imperfect, impermanent, and incomplete; about accepting complexity while at the same time valuing simplicity.

As we grow older, the idea of abandoning 'perfect' and accepting the scars and laugh lines seems increasingly prudent. Simplicity seems more appealing than forged exactness. This kind of shift can be truly liberating, and there's more than just beauty in it. If we can quieten our minds enough to appreciate the muted beauty of our lives, we are well on our way to practising *wabi-sabi*.

Shortly after turning forty, I had started noticing the deepening lines on my face and the puffiness under my eyes. Grey strands were showing up in my hair. I playfully started calling them my 'wisdom highlights'. Instead of spending hours in the salon, I chose to introspect and hone my skills. I figured that if I had something worthwhile to do as age crept up, a gratifying hobby or skill that I could share with the world, it would hold me in better stead. As one year folds into the next, I am glad about that decision. If I fail at something, instead of berating myself, I relax and try something else. That to me is 'looking at life through the *wabi-sabi* lens'.

In nature, everything is transient. A week ago, when the last of the *Ganesha* idols were being immersed, a discussion about its significance ensued over our evening tea. There are multiple theories about it, but one that interested me most was this: The idols initially were made out of the clay that formed on river beds. After the celebrations were over, those idols were returned to the river where they dissolved back into the water.

I thought about how this relates to our lives and it became even more important for me to celebrate the time I have here. I choose to put my energy into nurturing relationships and building a life I can be proud of. Growing old gracefully and joyfully is important. As Eleanor Roosevelt put is so correctly, "Beautiful young people are accidents of nature, but beautiful old people are works of art."

As for my dearest *paati*, I regrettably lost touch with her over the years. But her parting gift – a vintage bell – still hangs from a single nail on my bedroom wall. It is a reminder of the kind of person she was and the kind of person I wished I would eventually be. Simple, ordinary, and unapologetically beautiful in my own way.

THE SILENT STRING

In my early twenties, I was introduced to the stimulating music of the legendary Pandit Ravi Shankar. If I remember right, the album was called *Tana Mana – The Ravi Shankar Project*. It was an innovative experiment fusing electronic music with the traditional. And yet, the sitar stood out. The sound of that beautiful instrument mesmerized me. So much so, that I went in search of sitar classes in my neighbourhood. Much to my disappointment, things did not work out and my aspirations slowly got buried under more pressing concerns.

Even though I never learnt to play the sitar, I had done some research on the instrument at the time. One thing that stuck with me was the complex beauty of it. A sitar has 6-7 played strings and 18-21 sympathetic strings. The most used is the first string '*baaj ka taar*'. It is imperative to keep all the strings fine-tuned for perfect melody to flow out. The first string, though, is the anchor. It is on this string that the creative rendering of the ragas happens. But life is all about collaboration and balance. This is where the second string – the '*jod ka taar*' gains importance. That's the support string, without which continuity is lost and there can be no pure melody. The reason I'm eulogizing the sitar 20 years later is this:

Two weeks ago, while I was merrily cleaning out the kitchen shelves perched on a chair, I tripped and fractured my ankle. Life came to an excruciating standstill. Just a few weeks prior to this incident, I had written about meditation and being still; here was an opportunity to indulge in more of that. But there's a difference between elective choices and non-elective ones. Soon, annoyance and ennui crept in. The season of Advent had commenced and Christmas was just around the corner. It irked me that while everyone was decorating their homes, preparing sweets, and shopping, I had morphed into a kind of Hobbit, moping and shuffling around without shoes. So as I counted the similarities – no-shoes, six meals a day, and an unadventurous life, I read that Hobbits are also courageous under moral pressure and capable of great feats. It was time to slingshot the pessimism.

Fed on this last thought, I started an 'advent gratitude countdown' on Instagram and Facebook. I thought of every little thing that warranted thankfulness. Gratitude lists work so well for the simple reason that you can't feel thankful and sorry for yourself at the same time. Soon enough, I drew myself back into a bubble of appreciation and my mood brightened. The number of people who wrote back to me saying they drew comfort from my daily posts was a sweet incentive.

Gratitude to me is the most intense feeling and the only prayer I know of. Soon the frowns eased and I settled into a restorative state. The surest sign of blessings came soon after. My mother and husband both arrived home simultaneously, bringing with them lots of cheer and noise. It was the best dang thing. My husband kept everyone entertained, my daughter clowned around to replace him when he was at work, and mum pampered me like I was a baby. There is no bigger luxury than lovingly brewed tea brought to you in bed.

My adorable sister-in-law, Shalini, accompanied me on my doctor's visits and checked on me from time to time. Then there were friends, the real and honourable kinds. Some came with food, smiles, and hope. The ones who couldn't visit kept me occupied and positive via calls and text messages.

We imagine angels with halos and flowing white gowns, but good-hearted people are the real angels. They are the ones who radiate light and make our lives luminous. They are the ones who walk the talk. The words, laughter, encouragement, and love of these people became the crutch that I leaned on. They became my *'jod ka taar'*, the silent support string, without which no pure melody is possible. Appreciation exuded out of my every pore and made the days look like a perpetual sun-drenched morning. Sitting beneath my twinkling Christmas tree, I felt loved and sanctified by life. The best, as I always say, is always around the corner.

THAT THING YOU DO

Mr George, my English teacher in junior college, once caught me reading a novel during class. Instead of reprimanding me, he casually asked to see what I was hiding. "That's a great book you're reading," came his soft remark, "but I'd appreciate it if you continue with it after class." I was affected by his tact and kindness; needless to say, I never repeated the mistake. He proved that faults are best corrected with love. Once a week, Mr George would conduct 'rapid reading' sessions and he invariably picked me as the female lead each time. That was his way of encouraging my love for literature.

My love affair with books began at age seven when Dad gifted me a copy of *Snow White and the Seven Dwarfs*. It was a beautifully illustrated copy and took me to places I had never dreamed of. I realized there was another world beyond the tiny house I lived in, opening up infinite and off-beat possibilities.

While walking to school one day, I discovered a small library and sweet-talked mother into getting me a membership there. I treasured the laminated membership card like it was a ticket to paradise. Sure enough, the tiny store did turn out to be my wonderland where I dutifully lingered among the piles of vanilla-scented books once or twice a week.

Years later, when I discovered my flair for writing, it all went back to those sun-drenched words on interminable summer afternoons. It is strange that one should take that long to discover their aptitude, but better late than never. "People are strange. They are constantly angered by trivial things, but on a major matter like totally wasting their lives, they hardly seem to notice," wrote Charles Bukowski, the German-born American writer.

Now when I introduce myself as a writer, people ask how I found my passion. "I didn't really find it, it found me," I say. Discovering what you like isn't all that hard. Like kids being led by nothing but curiosity, you just go about doing whatever interests you. If you like it, you indulge in it; if not, you move on to the next thing. In my late twenties and all through my thirties, I dabbled in a lot of things. When you do something you like, your heart sings. So no one can say they don't know what their passion is. All you have to do is pay attention.

I first signed up for a creative writing course when I was working a nine-to-five job. My daughter was about five years old at the time. On my way back from work, I would pick her up from daycare, stop at the grocery, go home, tackle the housework, and end up exhausted. The only time I found in my chaotic day was my lunch break. So I would shut myself in one of the conference rooms for an hour and work on my assignments. Or I would read. The point is, when you truly enjoy something, you find time no matter how crazy your schedule.

I once asked a friend, a talented painter, why he doesn't paint anymore. He said his busy corporate life leaves him no free time. What I heard was this: That he is denying himself the one thing that defines him; the one thing that can restore him.

Jes Allen summed it up beautifully when she said, "That thing that you do, after your day job, in your free time, too early in the morning, too late at night. That thing you read about, write about, think about, in fact, fantasize about. That thing you do when you're all alone and there's no one to impress, nothing to prove, no money to be made, simply a passion to pursue. That's it. That's your thing. That's your heart, your guide. That's the thing you must, must do."

As for me, I love a lot of things. But the one activity I plan my day around is writing. Each morning, I can't wait to finish my chores so I can sit at my desk by the window, basking in the muted warmth of the sun, and let my words flow.

YOLO LEGACY

Sometime in the late 1930s, grandpa brought home a tiger cub. A fearless young lad at the time, he had spotted the lone cub, assumed it was abandoned, and decided to adopt it. Needless to say, he got a good scolding at home and was forced to return the cub to the forest. That was how grandpa was until the day he died – impulsive, adorable, and full of childlike curiosity.

Every summer, when it got too hot in the city, we packed our bags and went to live with grandpa and grandma. They lived in a modest home deep in the valleys of rural Mangalore in South India. That was our 'vacation'. It wasn't exotic but it was certainly enriching and pleasant. I adored grandpa and his idiosyncrasies.

The first thing he did every morning was to lovingly sweep the front yard. As soon as I woke up, he would hand me a small brass pot and take me to the well. We would draw water together, my small hands covered with his large, calloused ones over the rough rope. We would then water the garden and admire the flowers. While tending to the vegetable and fruit patch, he would point out the ripe ones and urge me to pick them. This is how he taught me to work joyously, to appreciate nature, to have patience, and enjoy the rewards when they appeared.

Once he hacked open a huge jack fruit with his bare hands and we chomped through the entire thing in one sitting. In today's lingo, it is called a "YOLO" day. A day when you indulge yourself because 'you only live once'. Grandpa lived and breathed the YOLO philosophy, though in a different way. It wasn't about pigging out on a certain day; it was living life to the fullest every single day. He exemplified how to nurture the inner child and never let it die.

On days that he chose to stay home, grandpa would sit out on the porch, listening to the news on his small portable radio. His sharp brain would absorb every bit of information and it was incredible how much he knew about world affairs. But, most days, he would disappear, only to appear in time for our evening prayers. He would waddle unconcerned down the dark, twisted path that led to our house in the valley. Grandma would keep expressing her disapproval about him being out so late, but he only just laughed all the time. Sometimes, he came home really late when we were already in bed. Then, he would squat on the mattress beside me, turn up the oil lamp a little, recount ghost stories in his booming voice, and sneak me sweets under the blanket while I hung on to his every word.

The way life has been pausing and crawling recently has given me new perspectives. Sometimes the rain falls around like it will never stop and, quite suddenly, the sun comes out and everything is so different. It's like living in two parallel universes. There are days when all I want to do is wear my escapist garb and crawl into my own skin. On days like that, a memory of grandpa and his toothless grin is enough to haul me back. And, quite suddenly things become symphonic and perfect. Life breaks free from shackles and appears untethered and free. There's a beauty in how relationships, past or present, are stitched together into our lives with 'invisible threads. How the seemingly simple can gain so much importance. Grandparents are always taken for granted but, someday, when they are gone, you realize that they live in parts of you that you didn't know existed. You then fall in love with reminiscences of them, as well as parts of you that they still live in.

Grandpa didn't accumulate wealth and heirlooms, but he loved life, indulged his curiosity, and laughed nonchalantly. Those are the qualities and lessons he seems to have passed on; a kind of legacy – the YOLO legacy, as I like to call it. What could be more precious than that? When I get excited about picking sea-shells from the shore, write poems on frosty window panes, lose myself in music, or laugh out loud at inane jokes, I think of grandpa. On dark days, when life seems to be pulling me down and I smile back at it, I hope he's proud of me. He never preached, but set us an example of how to feel wonder at the tiniest of things, how not to live a numb life, and how to open ourselves up to the wonder of 'us'.

AND SUDDENLY, YOU ARE HOME

I was raised in a small East-Indian community in suburban Mumbai. It was the perfect place to grow up in – simple, clean, and warm; all the things that define home for me. Our house was small but beautiful. There was a tiny patch right outside the window where mum used to grow roses, petunias, bougainvillaea, and some herbs. She would spend a lot of time tending to the plants. I did not understand all the effort she put into the activity at the time, but what mum was doing was pulling out the pesky weeds so her precious plants would have a healthy place to grow. When I was older, she explained to me that it isn't enough to just sow and water; frequent weeding is a priority if you want to see your garden thrive.

One recent autumn morning, walking down a street carpeted with fallen leaves, it occurred to me that like nature, we must periodically discard what's redundant too. More than the physical clutter, it's the mental mess that destroys us. Thoughts, feelings, and relationships need the most cleansing. People can either drain you until your veins feel dry or nourish you enough to make your soul sing. This is where mum's weeding theory came into play.

Last week, I visited Dubai. The glitz and glamour of the place never dazzled me even when I lived there for years. So what was it that bound me to this desert city? Why was I always eager to revisit?

There is a well-known and powerful Maori concept called *Turangawaewae*. Literally, *turanga* means "standing place" and *waewae* means "feet". So it translates as "a place to stand". *Turangawaewae* are places where we feel especially empowered and connected. They are our place in the world, our home. And home is always where your favourite people are.

That one week in Dubai was beautiful beyond words. Every meal was shared with people that mattered, every sunrise nurtured those bonds, and every sunset sealed them. On my flight back to Mumbai, I came across this beautiful summation of 'home' by K.R.R. that summed it all up: "It's fascinating how we're taught that 'home' is this tangible place, the most simply defined to terms – it's a house, a postcode, a country. And yet, sometimes home cannot be explained by a street number; sometimes it's a face, a voice, a laugh more honest and familiar than any truth you have ever known. We're taught that in its most literal sense, home is where we live and grow. But, one day, in the silence that follows nostalgic stories and subsequent laughter, you may realize that you never did more living or growing than when you had certain people by your side. And suddenly, you are home."

SIMPLE SUSTENANCE

During the summer of 1984, I had my first experience of community cooking. In those days, weddings in Mangalore were a long-drawn-out affair that lasted days and brought the whole neighbourhood together. Food was organic, authentic, and cooked in huge cauldrons on open wood fires.

It was a twin wedding in the family, so we were doubly excited. The evening before the wedding, insane amounts of soaked rice and lentils were ground manually on huge grinding stones and left to ferment for *idlis* to be made the next morning. I chose to be on the *idli*-makers team and woke up at the crack of dawn to assist. The aromas, the exuberance, the solidarity of it all, are lodged as a surreal kind of remembrance in my mind.

In retrospect, my whole life seems like a roaring compilation of food memories. In the tiny home I grew up in, there was no separate kitchen to speak of. From the *divan*, which was my self-proclaimed throne, I could just reach out to the cooking counter. Mum used to wake up early and start working on the *chapatis* and omelettes. That's the aroma I would wake up to. As I grew up, I was eager to lend a hand. Mum and I would work side by side in the minuscule space, singing along to the radio. To this day, we bond best when we are cooking together. Like two comrades, we embark upon adventures with our new recipes, get delirious with the difficult ones, and find quietude in the tried and tested. When we're done feasting, we go on walks, she talking incessantly about this and that and making me laugh until suddenly, we're back to discussing our next meal.

The neighbourhood I grew up in was a different world altogether. Walking unannounced into each other's homes for a meal was very normal. The Koltes next door was a family of six. Mrs Kolte was a great cook. Though they didn't have much, she managed to put together meals that could compete with that of a professional chef. I just have to close my eyes, think of her spicy chicken gravy served with mixed lentil *vadas,* and I'm transported back to her home. On special occasions, she would always send us food before she fed her own family. It was neighbourly love on a level that doesn't exist anymore.

Then there was Aunt Gertie. She was a kitchen elf who chose to spend all her free time baking and cooking. On the days that she made crabs, I would shamelessly hover around until she asked me to stay for dinner. Then I would sit cross-legged in her kitchen and savour the meal in a rapturous state, unaware of the crab juice running down my arms. She would point me out to her daughter, Sheryll, who was my best friend and say, "This is how you eat. Stop picking at your food and learn something from the girl!"

One day, I surprised our house-help, Barki, with a strange request. She lived in a tiny hut just across the lane. Every evening as the sun went down, she would squat in front of an open fire and make piles of *jowar bhakris* to feed her large family. That day, I asked if I could join them for dinner. She was aghast and didn't know how to respond. It mortified her to think that all she had to offer was *jowar bhakris,* bland *dal* and a chilli-garlic chutney. But, to me, it was enough. The smell of burning wood, the bite of the chutney, the fresh-off-the-fire bread, the cool winter breeze, and the happy tears in my host's eyes made it one of the most memorable meals I'd ever had.

From the *kulfiwala* who fed us free *kulfis* after school, to the grocer who packed a few extra dates as a treat, the love far exceeded everything else. Later, when I entered the cold corporate world, the only solace amidst the chaos of pounding typewriter keys and mounds of paperwork was the lunch break. I've always been fortunate to find people who make it their business to feed me. My first job was in a huge organization where, to my utter surprise, the cooks took an instant liking to me and singled me out for attention. The food they cooked was only for the top management, but they sneaked me into the pantry and fed me meals that smelled and tasted like *manna* from heaven.

When I moved to Dubai, the pantry experience moved with me. Only the cuisine differed. I was working with Iranians there and found a new kind of food paradise. Regardless of whether I had carried a meal-box from home or not, the cook would send steaming trays of *cheelo kebabs*, feta cheese, Iranian bread, and salads every afternoon. One day, I got them tandoori chicken as a return gesture. My Iranian bosses ate it with gusto but the spice was too much for them. The fair Iranians had sweat dripping and tears streaming down their reddened faces!

Dubai was all about food and friends. Every weekend was a big pot-luck party. In the winter months, we would carry huge amounts of marinated meat to a park or beach and enjoy barbecues. We sat around the glowing embers and devoured juicy chunks of chicken and sausages with Arabic bread, hummus, and pickles. The camaraderie of those cool winter evenings in a foreign land was an experience beyond words. It was like huddling together under a warm blanket.

Whether it is luscious fruits in the heat of Bangkok, chilled coconut water in the quiet streets of Phuket, warm *shawarmas* on the way to Hatta or sizzling *falafels* in the mountains of Oman, the key ingredient of a good meal is the simplicity with which it is cooked, served, and eaten. The best *parantha* I have ever eaten was at a rickety *dhaba* on the Delhi-Agra highway. It was served with a dollop of white butter and a kind smile. The most sumptuous Maharashtrian meal I remember is at a small resort in Sogaon, served by a sincere, loving hand.

Modern life has altered the eating experience for most of us. But every now and then, I like to make the food and memories count. Since we choose friends that resonate with who we are, my flock was, is, and always will be a bunch of foodies. We discuss food as if our life depends on it. We eat like there is no tomorrow. It isn't gluttony, but an expression of who we are.

The way I see it, the sharing of a meal is as emotionally and spiritually nurturing as the food on our plates. It is what rejuvenates and bonds us. It is pure sustenance. My food experiences, intertwined with my relationships, have defined the way I view life. There are lots of parallels to draw. But one that I uphold above everything else whether it is food, friendship, or life is this: That simplicity trumps everything.

OHANA

The house looked poured out, empty. For over a week, it was bursting at the seams. Faces radiant, rooms buzzing, bodies moving and colliding, bags stacked against walls, chaos everywhere. There were moments when people were talking all at once and raucous laughter bounced off walls. Family from overseas had arrived home to celebrate the 75th birthday of the family matriarch. Some days are just hallowed and we had a week full of them.

It's a fact that no matter how much you try, distance makes relationships come undone a little, or totally sometimes. You send messages, make calls on special occasions, and try your best to hold everything together. But sharing meals cooked together in large old pots, kitchen gossip over cups of tea, or watching the kids huddled up on makeshift beds, these are things that pull a family together like nothing else can. What started off as a birthday celebration became the glue that bonded us all back together. We manifested magic in those few days.

As expected, the birthday party was spectacular. The day shone with epic moments and sparkling tributes.

There was singing, dancing, and a lot of warm hugs. Mother-in-law, whom everyone, young and old, fondly calls 'Mai' (which means 'mother' in Konkani), was beaming the whole time. Seven kids, their spouses, ten grandkids, extended family, close friends; the vibrations that filled that banquet hall were incredible. These are the memories that fill your heart; the ones you talk to posterity about.

Everyone has long returned to their homes and I am settled into my world, but there are moments when I miss them. The first couple of days, I wandered around in a daze, unsure of how to go back to normalcy. My sister-in-law left behind the kids' cereal box and bowls and I let them sit where she left them on my kitchen counter. Little parts of them that made me feel they were still around. When people come into your world, even for a short while, they leave remnants. Little smatterings that make everything look different. I don't know when days like these will return, but there's hope that what we sowed will bloom time and again. So, now in moments of solitude, I silently send up a prayer to good times – the ones we enjoyed and the ones foreseen. Until then, there's a fountain of reminiscences to soak in.

There were lots of precious moments, but one memory stands out for me. My nine-year-old niece, Keira, all dressed to leave for the airport, was stirring random chocolaty things that she picked from my larder and refrigerator in a warm bowl. I asked her what she was doing and she replied, "I'm making you a dessert before I leave. This is just for you." It was so incredibly charming that my heart melted faster than the chocolate in that red bowl. There was so much purity and affection in that little gesture. Keira gave me an intense, beautiful memory to hold for life.

In Hawaiian culture, '*ohana*' means family. The term was made famous in the movie 'Lilo & Stitch'. There is a scene where Stitch is running away and Lilo in her soft, heartrending voice says: "*Ohana* means family. Family means 'no one gets left behind'. But if you want to leave, you can. I'll remember you though." That's what I want to say. To Keira, my 'Stitch', and the rest of the family as well. That whether we are together or separated by oceans, we must make sure that we do not forget and no one gets left behind. Here's to *Ohana*. To family.

A LEGACY OF LOVE

Reveries are good, but you can't stay there forever. All week, I'd been waiting for inspiration. Something, anything, to rouse and stir me. The days weren't empty, far from it; yet there were gaps. Lacklustre little gaps that struggled to let the light in; that demanded more. As the seasons moved, I recognized the need for alteration and change.

So, it seemed appropriate that my sister-in-law suggested a trip to the tranquil Fr. Agnel's church in Bandra, to commemorate Papa's fifth death anniversary. Tucked away from the bustle of the city, the timeworn church sits serenely amidst sounds of birds and the sea. Inside, the air is old and dark and luminous all at once. You feel primal and pristine. Ancient, yet improved. It's the kind of place where you reclaim yourself. Later, we visited The Shanti Avedna Cancer Home, a few blocks away. I was reluctant to go at first, but it turned out to be one of the most calming places I have ever visited. Peace and love grace those quiet hallways; abundantly so, and certainly enough to alter a little something inside you.

I don't know why exactly my sister-in-law chose these two places, but once I went there, they took on significance for me. Both the places matched Papa's personality. Sturdy and serene. Quiet and assertive. And, most of all, filled to the brim with love. Four years ago, on his first death anniversary, I had tried to encapsulate Papa's substantial life story into a few words.

This is probably how inspiration is found. In little things, in modest lives, in unpretentious people. So, here I am, repeating that same story. Maybe it will touch you and stimulate you. Maybe it will take care of your gaps. Maybe it will just remind you of things you have forgotten. And, in reminding you, I will reminisce myself.

This is the story of Papa, my father-in-law. A man I'm proud to have known.

It was towards the end of 2009 that Papa got diagnosed with throat cancer. He was old and not very strong physically, but he had an amazing strength of mind. When we told him the doctors had advised radiation, he just accepted it without question or complaint. I do not know another person who has borne such intense pain with so much dignity and silence.

The agony went on for days. And then, God decided that a man so gallant deserved to be in a better place. Just as the sun went down on Monday, the 23rd of November, 2009, Papa moved on to a higher life.

Anyone who knew Papa would agree that he was one of a kind; a man of great integrity, honesty, and self-respect. He raised seven wonderful children in his lifetime, saw them settle down into their careers and marriages, enjoyed his ten grandkids, and celebrated everything with a cryptic smile on his face. Since he spoke very little, he was never the centre of attraction; but his presence and his personality always stood out even in the midst of a crowd.

Many people find it hard to believe when told by his very successful children, that Papa had been a taxi driver all his life. Those were times of extreme hardship and abject poverty. If he took even a single day off, the family was affected. So, Papa worked every single day, come rain or thunderstorm. One thing always struck me tremendously and it still does. Whenever my husband or his siblings speak about their seemingly deprived childhood, they only have positive and happy memories. How could they have been so content, I wondered, when they had so little? No fancy home, no branded clothes, no colourful toys ... and yet their childhood had been filled with laughter and love. Papa couldn't provide them with expensive things, but he gave them love, family ties, and values which have held them in good stead to this day.

Papa left us with many valuable lessons, precious memories, and a legacy of love, family bonding, and integrity. The day after his burial, we all sat late into the night talking about what we learnt from him. And the lessons were many; not only from his life but from his death as well. Even in death, Papa brought his family closer.

For more than a week afterwards, when we clung together supporting each other, we questioned ourselves, talked endlessly, strengthened our bonds, ate and prayed together, and made little resolutions in our hearts to love and live well.

Life knows and it tells us more than we care to understand. Not many of us think of death while we are busy living. But when we lose someone dear to us, God might be sending us a reminder. A reminder to pause in the midst of all the chaos, go within and find our essence.

MICHELANGELIC

When I was in school, someone gifted me a kaleidoscope. I remember being quite enamoured by the uniqueness of the toy. The science behind it escaped me at the time, but the fascination lasted for quite a while. If you think about it, all a kaleidoscope contains is angled mirrors and little bits of coloured objects. But the patterns alter depending on the movement, and light that infiltrates through the other end. That's how life is too – little things coming together to form patterns. But what's important is to 'let the light in'.

Of late, my words are slow to come. I go from staring uncomprehendingly into voids to thinking too much; thoughts either stagnant or threatening to gush out incoherently. I've been aching for serenity, for unflustered reflections and deliberate actions. For a culmination of the bipolarity of my two selves – one that finds the exotic in the ordinary and the other that looks for familiarity in the unknown. I long to step out of the dark and find my own radiance.

As November moved forward, I started yearning more and more for a throwback to calm days. Days when

I could sit still and luxuriate in nothing but my own skin. My yoga days that I had left behind, now beckoned to me. So I pulled out my old blue mat and tried to meditate. Meditation is unbeatable in its simplicity, but don't be fooled into thinking that it's easy. Thoughts cascade and hurtle across like an avalanche over you. A few days into it and things start getting better; until you reach a point where everything stands absolutely still.

Life is always a work-in-progress. You build some and crumble some. And, sometimes, you have to assemble yourself from scratch. There's much to learn from every experience and every person you encounter, even toddlers. Recently, I teamed up with my three-year-old nephew, Ethan, in a bid to encourage his new passion – colouring. It was surreal, the way we bonded over rhythmically moving crayons, not just with each other, but with our own selves. And just like that, I discovered a new way to meditate.

I don't believe in coincidences, so a couple of days later, when my daughter introduced me to *Mandala* colouring pages for adults, I knew there was a connection. This was a new way to deconstruct and interpret pre-determined notions. As I poured colour into the intricate designs, it was like creating a self-portrait, understated and pure. *Mandala*, which means 'circle' in Sanskrit, is a spiritual symbol representing the universe. A simple geometric shape that has no beginning or end, much like space or our own abiding souls. I loved the purity of the experience. Whatever the endeavour, our triumphs depend on our openness to receive and grow.

Life is fickle; proof of it was the November rain that poured out of unrelenting skies onto bewildered heads two nights ago. It's amazing if you're prepared for such impulsiveness. If not, it does well to go with the flow and enjoy yourself. That's how the kaleidoscope of life works. That is how the light gets in. So we, my daughter and I, got home completely drenched and made quite an evening of it with hot baths, a couple of warm drinks, steaming food, an animated exchange of stories, and an old Hollywood classic on television. Evenings like that are ephemeral and not to be wasted. They're like visiting old childhood haunts that leave one replete.

So, at the end of all the meditation, whether it was by sitting still or decanting colour into monochromatic patterns, valuable realizations emerged. That there is a season for everything. For rushing around and for slowing down. That self-discovery can come from the most inconspicuous of experiences. That once we let the light in, life can be beautiful from every angle. All we need to do is relentlessly work at discovering our real selves. When Michelangelo was applauded for the magnificence of David's statue, all he said was this: "David was always there in the marble. I just took away everything that was not David." This is what Shifrah Combiths describes as 'Michelangelic' – the beauty that's left when everything that doesn't belong is chipped away.

LAGOM

Life is defined not by apocalyptic moments, but from diminutive ones that come forth like a whisper. One of my most defining moments came in September of 2000 – the day I decided to quit my job. We were expatriates in a foreign land but I never felt like an outsider there. The work was alright too. It's just that my heart wasn't in it. I was working for an Iranian family business. They were nice people and treated me well. No late sitting, never a harsh word, and authentic Iranian food served for lunch. My love for Chelo Kebabs and Bademjan have stood the test of time. Yet, there was a discontent I couldn't quite explain.

It wasn't an easy decision to make. For starters, I was throwing away my financial independence. It meant cutting down on a lot of things. But I was firm. Too much money was never a goal. The Swedish have a word for it – *Lagom*. It means something like, not too much, not too little, but just right. So I went ahead and did what felt right. In all the years since I have never regretted my decision. What I gained was way more than what I lost. Among other important things, spending precious time with my daughter was and remains the most rewarding experience.

By then, I was already on my way to discovering my passion – writing. I took up little projects and opportunities that came my way. It didn't pay me much, but being true to myself and doing that which pleased me was compensation enough. Each day, I was becoming more and more the kind of person I liked. As opposed to a salary that earlier defined my worth, I was now discovering that my true worth came from the peace and joy that I radiated. Choosing work that makes you show up even if it's unpaid is what defines your true path. Besides, when you do what you love abundance follows.

This thought was amplified recently when I visited the slums of Govandi, the dumping ground of Mumbai. It's a poverty-stricken, crime-riddled place. There is garbage piled sky-high, the homes are little more than tin roofs and bare floors, there is never enough food and, worst of all, the water supply comes from tankers 'once a week'. Domestic violence, addictions, rapes, and incest are rampant.

In the midst of this ramshackle world, a friend of mine runs a school for the slum kids. These kids come from the lowest strata of society, from below the so-called poverty line. Their stark stories were sordid enough to outdo the dump that bordered their world. But, despite all that, the first thing you notice is the sparkle in their eyes! Their eagerness to study, to move forward, to earn their rightful place in society shines in those beautiful faces. At home, they might be just another pair of hands that rummage through garbage to earn some money. But in that dilapidated building that housed their classroom, they were transformed. Life sprang forth from them like rainbows from a sun-drenched monsoon sky.

Later, as we walked around the *basti*, a little girl started following us around like a lamb. Along the way, Nazia slipped her hand into mine. It was a casual gesture but somehow it meant the world to me. It was more than just a holding of hands; it spoke of trust, hope, and connection.

Sometimes, the Universe sends us pay-checks; and sometimes a bonus. I recognized the day as a blessing. In a society, where everyone is constantly trying to prove something to the world and is hankering after more and more, I was introduced to selflessness, compassion, empathy, and pure love. The teachers and staff who work there come from poor families too, but they look like the richest people in the world. They radiate a glow that comes from compassion and selfless love. Their life is a daily struggle to educate those kids, yet they look serene. All they seem to want is a little help and support. Not too much, not too little, but just right. Like the Swedish say, '*Lagom*'.

THE VAGUS NERVE

2019 was a year of striking contrasts. On the one hand, I finally got my first book of poems published. The appreciation and love that poured in put me in a many-hued reverie. On the other hand, I was decidedly neglecting my health and ended up feeling listless all the time. Wasn't I the one who always reprimanded people on valuing material gifts, but abusing their own bodies, the most precious gift that life bestows on us? Somehow, my innate wisdom had abandoned me, returning to survey the damage a little too late.

There's a Japanese phrase '*Kuchisabishii*', which means "when you're not hungry, but you eat because your mouth is lonely." At some point or the other, we are prone to emotional eating and drinking, but when indulgence becomes a habit, it is a cause for concern. It is a sign that something is wrong at a deeper level. Thankfully, life provides a U-turn on most paths. Now, I'm bringing the focus back on wellness; exercising, trying to eat sensibly, and, most importantly, regaining the mental calm that is imperative to stay on the path.

In hindsight, this year certainly proved to be the perfect teacher, stern and relentless in its lessons but compassionate and fair too. There were times when the ground beneath my feet seemed to be slipping when nothing gave me hope and my otherwise radiant smile seemed totally jaded. Just in time though, some good karma found its way back.

Recently, while listening to a podcast, I learnt about the 'Vagus nerve', the so-called 'nerve of emotion'. It is the largest cranial nerve that relays messages between the brain and the respiratory, digestive, and nervous systems. It is this neural pathway that determines your ability to find calm by activating the 'relaxation response', thus decreasing stress and inflammation, the underlying cause of all disease. It has now become clear to me why yogic practices such as pranayama and meditation are so important. Establishing an optimal vagal tone should be our top priority in this increasingly stressful world that we live in.

Another way to improve your vagal tone is to train yourself to experience life mindfully and practice a sense of oneness. Just living in the moment, laughing without restraint, experiencing loving relationships, feeling gratitude, and connecting with nature are some easy ways to do so. Allow joy, love, and calm to steadily permeate you.

December is always about an easy, magical buildup to Christmas and a brand new year. The twinkling fairy lights are the best mood-setters and just sitting by the Christmas tree, listening to cheery songs makes me feel grateful for all the little blessings received. It is also the perfect time for slowing down, reflecting on the year gone by, and making changes.

If you ask me to summate my year's worth of learning into one word, I'd say, 'serve'. Make a contribution. As a writer, touching a heart with words of hope, reminding someone to appreciate the little things, and sharing personal experiences that others can gain some insight from, seems a good place to start. The upside of this is that when you unwaveringly focus on being your best self, the futility just falls off. Each choice you make creates a ripple effect and consequently affects the lives of others. A kind heart, a clear mind, and dedicated work can be your best service to humankind. Everyone has a purpose, find yours.

THE QUARANTINE OF 2020

Every morning, for days now, I've been observing the process and patience of nature. As I sit by the window sipping tea, my gaze is fixed on the Yellow-flame tree outside. A pair of egrets had built a nest and soon I spotted three little heads popping through the branches. It was a joy to see new life. However, what interested me was how beautifully unhurried and serene the process was. They say life doesn't come with a manual, but it does. Just look around.

2020 has been nothing short of revolutionary so far. It has brought humankind down on its knees in the most unprecedented way. One after the other, countries have gone into lockdown owing to the dreaded Covid-19. This must be the first time in history that everyone is, quite literally, in the same boat and speaking the same language. Status, hierarchy, religious differences, everything has melted away, at least for now. People are more compassionate and empathetic towards each other.

When the lockdown was announced in India, the collective panic of the nation was felt like a tangible thing.

I felt it too, but only for a few minutes. It is important that fear, sooner than later, gives way to acceptance.

Back in school, I remember painting a motivation card and placing it on the television set. It read: "Hope for the best, be prepared for the worst." This quote had a profound effect on me. People might see me as an idealist, but for the longest time, I've built myself on the idea of acceptance. When faced with a dire situation, my first question is: "What is the worst that can happen and how will I handle that?" It instantly calms me down, because I realise that life doesn't give us anything we can't handle. In any difficult situation, allow yourself to feel the fear and panic fully, let it rattle you, then take a deep breath and think about how you can best handle it.

A friend recently asked me how we can maintain hope and optimism in the midst of such tremendous panic. The quarantine of 2020 has given us a lot to reconsider: how we live our lives, how we must conduct ourselves, what is really important, what are our strengths and weaknesses, how we can rearrange ourselves, and how we must use technology to our advantage.

The onslaught of conflicting information is overwhelming. The loss of life is disturbing. So, my first step was to cut out unnecessary information and focus on things that sustained me. That done, it has been heartening to see how human spirits shine during a crisis. There is so much to learn. If we eschew the victim mentality and adopt a warrior mindset, we are bound to win.

Lent, for the past couple of years, has been a significant time for me. This year, once churches closed down, schedules got disrupted. But the season turned out to be more profound than usual. We realised so much in a short time. People who matter, the ones who care about you, and the ones you worry about. The frivolity of titles and luxuries seem less important when we realise that all we need to survive are essentials. Above all, there is deep gratitude for all that we have received in abundance. Nature has provided us with so much, but it is only when our breath is threatened by a virus that we recognise the blessings we have taken for granted.

Let us not blame anyone or demand proof of a God that we can relate to only by faith. We are called human 'beings', so all we essentially need to do is learn how to 'be'. Let us stop running around and slow down.

After all the signs, do we, who call ourselves educated and thinking people, need more proof? We don't know yet when the crisis will end, but nothing lasts forever and this too shall pass. However, and this is important, let us never lose faith.

EPILOGUE

As I celebrate another chapter of my earnest and quiet life, this little book constitutes a toast to all that I'm grateful for. To me, what enables an impassioned, bonafide life is the people who grace it.

My friend, Gazala, once wrote about how they nurtured their bashful little orchid plant that refused to flower. It took a year and a half of coaxing and whispering sweet-nothings for a beautiful white orchid to finally bloom. That's how people are too; you dust them with rhythmic sprinklings of love and they flourish.

I have many people to thank. Firstly, doting family and some vintage friends who have stuck on. Then there are the inspiring ones who come in with fresh perspectives, sometimes for a reason, sometimes for a season. The strangeness and magnificence of life are authenticated by all these associations.

As I write this, I draw solace from the flowering of the Gulmohar tree outside my window. The Gulmohar brings back memories of a distant childhood when we used to play under its fiery red canopy and wait for its long seed cases to turn brown and hard, so we could rattle

Epilogue

them all day. But what really makes it precious to me is an allegory that I have dearly held on to for years: that the flowering of this bountiful tree coincides with my birthday for a reason. I see it as Nature's gift to me; a reminder that when the summers of life get unbearable, there is always a burst of hope to cling on to. That even as life hurts me, it hands me the idea that I inherently possess the grace to find my own fluorescence.

Despite my polychromatic weaknesses, I have come a long way. I am beholden to all who walk with me and lend a hand to help me execute this sometimes dark, sometimes sparkling life with a poise that can only come from genuine love. Here's hoping you feel grateful for every little blessing in your life too.